Thumbody Loves You

Dedication:

Thanks be to God for the inspiration!

Written by Barbara Pierson

Illustrated by Charlo Nocete

Thumbody

is you

Written by **Barbara Pierson**

Illustrated by Charlo Nocete

Order this book online at www.trafford.com
or email orders@trafford.com

Most Trafford titles are also available at major online book retailers.

Printed in the United States of America.

ISBN: 978-1-4251-3101-2

Trafford rev. 07/05/2011

 www.trafford.com

North America & international
toll-free: 1 888 232 4444 (USA & Canada)
phone: 250 383 6864 ♦ fax: 812 355 4082

Miss Thumb One walked briskly up the walk to the Thumbody's house. She couldn't stop wondering to herself, "Did I do the right thing in calling those two? Will they come to the picnic? Should I call them back?"

Miss Thumb One was now at the door of the house, so she knocked and then waited patiently on the front step.

Pop Thumbody was sitting in his chair thumbing through the Thumb Times Newspaper when he heard the knock. He hastened to open the front door.

"Hello, Miss Thumb One," said Pop.

"Hello, Mr. Thumbody," said Miss Thumb One. "How are you today?"

"Just fine," replied Pop. "Come on in."

"Thank you."

"Are you ready for the picnic?" asked Pop.

"Oh, yes. I look forward to this event every year. I always have the best time," said Miss Thumb One. "Is everyone ready to go?"

"Hello, Miss Thumb One," said Mother Thumbody as she bristled about packing baby bottles for her baby quinthumplets and making certain she had everything they needed for the picnic. These five babies were really quite a handful.

"Hello, Mother Thumbody. Can you use a hand?" offered Miss Thumb One.

"Well, I think everything is ready," quipped Mother Thumbody.

Just as she spoke, however, Mother spied Baby Thumbody getting ready to go outside. "Wait, Baby," she said. "You need some lotion. We certainly don't want you to get a thumburn."

Miss Thumb One took the lotion, and said, "I'll do that for you." She took the Thumtan lotion and rubbed it all over Baby Thumbody's exposed face and arms. "You'll probably be in the thumbshine most of the day, but you should be fine now," smiled Miss Thumb One.

After she had thoroughly lathered Baby Thumbody with the lotion, she said, "Baby, please put Brownie outside because we are ready to go."

"OK," said Baby Thumbody. He held the door open and called his pet lion, "Here, Brownie." The little Lion Thumbody bounded into the kitchen and straight out the door into the backyard.

Miss Thumb One peeked out the door and saw Mr. Green Thumb, the gardener, had just finished mowing the grass. He took excellent care of the yard. The hedges were neatly trimmed, the trees pruned, and flowers flourished all around the house. Thumble bees buzzed from blossom to blossom.

Mr. Green Thumb approached the back door and informed Mother Thumbody, "I'm finished for the day, so I'll see you at the picnic."

"Great," said Mother Thumbody. "See you there."

Miss Thumb One smiled at Mr. Green Thumb and waved goodbye. She returned to the kitchen, grabbed the baby carriage with the five baby thumbs, and wheeled it into the living room. "All present and accounted for," she said as she stood in military fashion saluting Pop Thumbody.

"Excellent, soldier," said Pop as he returned the salute and opened the door. He stood aside, and snapped, "Company! Atten...tion! Forward, march!"

Miss Thumb One put on a serious face, stood stiffly, then marched forward with the quints in the baby carriage, followed by a marching Mother and Baby.

Miss Thumb One and the family laughed as they all finally shuffled into the van.

As Pop drove to their destination, Miss Thumb One talked about a special project she had undertaken for her senior high school science class regarding thumbs who were once hard as nails, but now were suffering with the dreaded nail ridges. Those thumbs had practically disappeared from society and were rarely heard from.

Pop Thumbody drove to Thumb Place where the Annual Thumb Day Picnic was held. It seemed almost every thumb in town had turned up for this gala event.

The quinthumplets were the pride of the town, so everyone assisted with their care. Mother Thumbody was really happy to get so many helping hands.

After seeing that the quints were well cared for, Miss Thumb One started mingling with the other thumbs at the picnic. As she ventured around, Miss Thumb One observed Fear Thumb and Grue Thumb sitting under a tree far away from everyone else. She smiled and immediately ran over to the awethumb twothumb. "Good afternoon, Mr. Fear Thumb and Mr. Grue Thumb."

"Good afternoon, Miss Thumb One," said Fear Thumb with a smile.

"Good afternoon, Miss Thumb One," said Grue Thumb.

"I'm so happy that you both came. I wasn't certain that you would when I called and invited you. May I join you?" she inquired.

"You are a very polished young lady, and I'm sure you would rather spend your time with someone other than us," said Fear Thumb.

"I'm quite certain I will enjoy your company," said Miss Thumb One as she sat down beside him. "Like I told you when we talked, you don't have to be ashamed just because you have ridges. Those who thumbed their noses at you are the ones who should be ashamed.

And I know, once bitten, twice shy, but if you ever

see them again, you just tell them to take a hike. You've

hidden yourself from people for so long, that everyone

has practically forgotten who you are. You've been blue

long enough, so let's get you back in the pink.

The three thumbs were soon laughing and talking. They played and talked for thumbtime. After a while, Miss Thumb One grabbed the twothumb and took them over to the other thumbs. She introduced them to the quinthumplets.

"The two boys are Berry Thumbody and Hairy Thumbody, and the three girls are Carry Thumbody, Marry Thumbody, and Sherry or Share Thumbody for short.

Pop Thumbody gave the two shy thumbs a hardy handshake. "Any friend of Miss Thumb One is a friend of mine," he said smiling.

Mother Thumbody also gave the two a warm smile as she shook their hands.

The other thumbs shied away initially, but then recalled who the awethumb twothumb were. Soon all were having a good time recalling old times with Fear and Grue.

Miss Thumb One reintroduced them to Twiddle Dee Thumb, the town tailor who custhumbized all the Thumb Wear, and was thoroughly delighted to see his designs sported at the picnic.

Even Worry Thumb, who always seemed to be thumbwhat anxious about everything, appeared to relax around the two.

Thumpkin Head welcomed the two back and then continued looking for a handout.

The girls surrounding Hands Thumb stopped giggling and flirting long enough to talk with the two.

Thumb Teachers, who taught the Rules of Thumb in school, introduced themselves.

Adventure Thumb sat with a group of children boasting of his journeys and conquests, and invited Fear Thumb and Grue Thumb to join them.

"Thank you, Miss Thumb One," said Grue Thumb. "Thumbhow, thumbway, I know your kindness will be repaid."

Miss Thumb One blushed, "I didn't do anything special. You two did all of the hard work by overcoming your fears, and getting back into the swing of things."

Fear Thumb and Grue Thumb joined Adventure Thumb.

Miss Thumb One beamed as she saw the two thumbs

enjoying themselves. She started back to the quints,

when suddenly, a handsthumb gentleman approached her.

Miss Thumb One's heart pounded rapidly in her chest.

She couldn't believe her eyes. It was Thumb Prince!

Their eyes met. He stared at her the same way she stared

at him. It was love at first sight.

Thumb Prince walked over to Miss Thumb One and gazed gently into her eyes.

"I don't believe we ever met. My name is Tom."

"Hello, Tom. I'm Miss Thumb One."

"I couldn't help but notice you, and how you befriended Fear Thumb and Grue Thumb," said Tom.

"Their ridges have caused them to look a little different than most of us, but the same thing could happen to any one of us. Then too, we can't judge people solely by the way they look," said Miss Thumb One.

"That is true. I admire you very much for offering your friendship to thumone no others would even talk to."

The rest is history. Miss Thumb One had nailed the Prince. The two dated through the remainder of their senior year, and the day finally came when the two were married.

The couple lived happily ever after, even though they had just one little thumb thing after another.